The Farmer's Away! BAA! NEIGH!

arf

yap

baa

neigh

mew

quack

cluck

moo

mama

splish

splash

honk

tweet

cheep

bzz

sss

oink

ree

ribbet

eek

cock-a-doodle-doo

For Dad,
who taught me the importance of silliness
and for Aaron,
who carries on the tradition

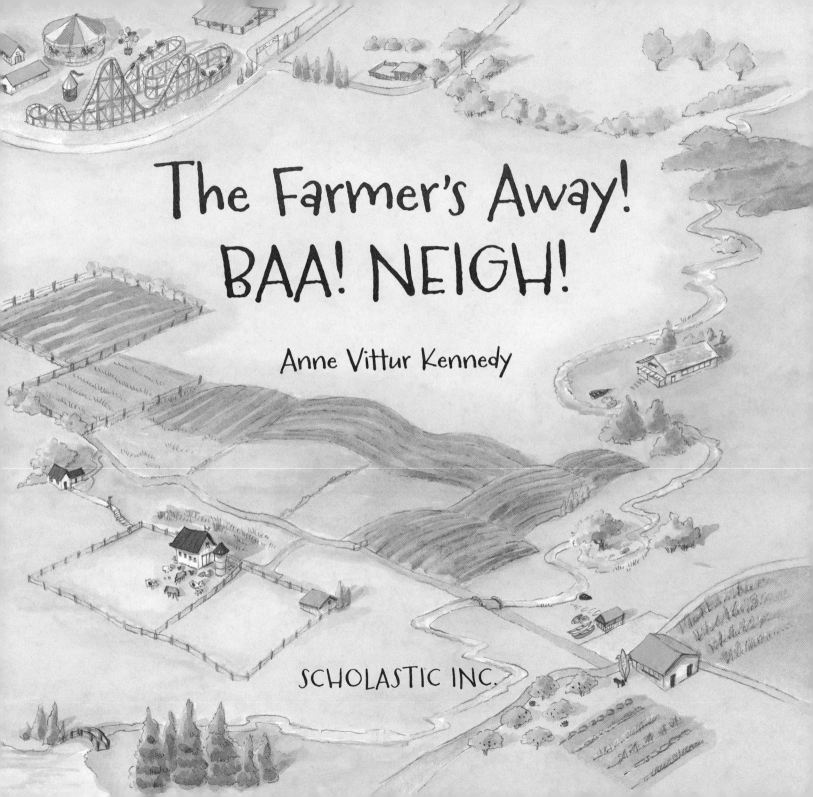

The Farmer's Away!
BAA! NEIGH!

Anne Vittur Kennedy

SCHOLASTIC INC.

ribbet mama ribbet mama
eek honk quack

splish splash baa baa
moo moo yap

arf neigh cluck cluck
cock-a-doodle-doo

mama mew mama mew
splish neigh moo

sss sss sss sss
yap sss eek

bzz bzz bzz bzz
quack bzz tweet

cock-a-doodle-doo moo
ribbet ribbet sss

baa cheep baa cheep
oink oink bzz

hmm . . . hmm . . .

neigh arf neigh moo
mew mew mew

oink ree ree ree
cock-a-doodle-doo

neigh neigh baa baa
moo moo tweet

honk honk oink oink
arf cheep eek

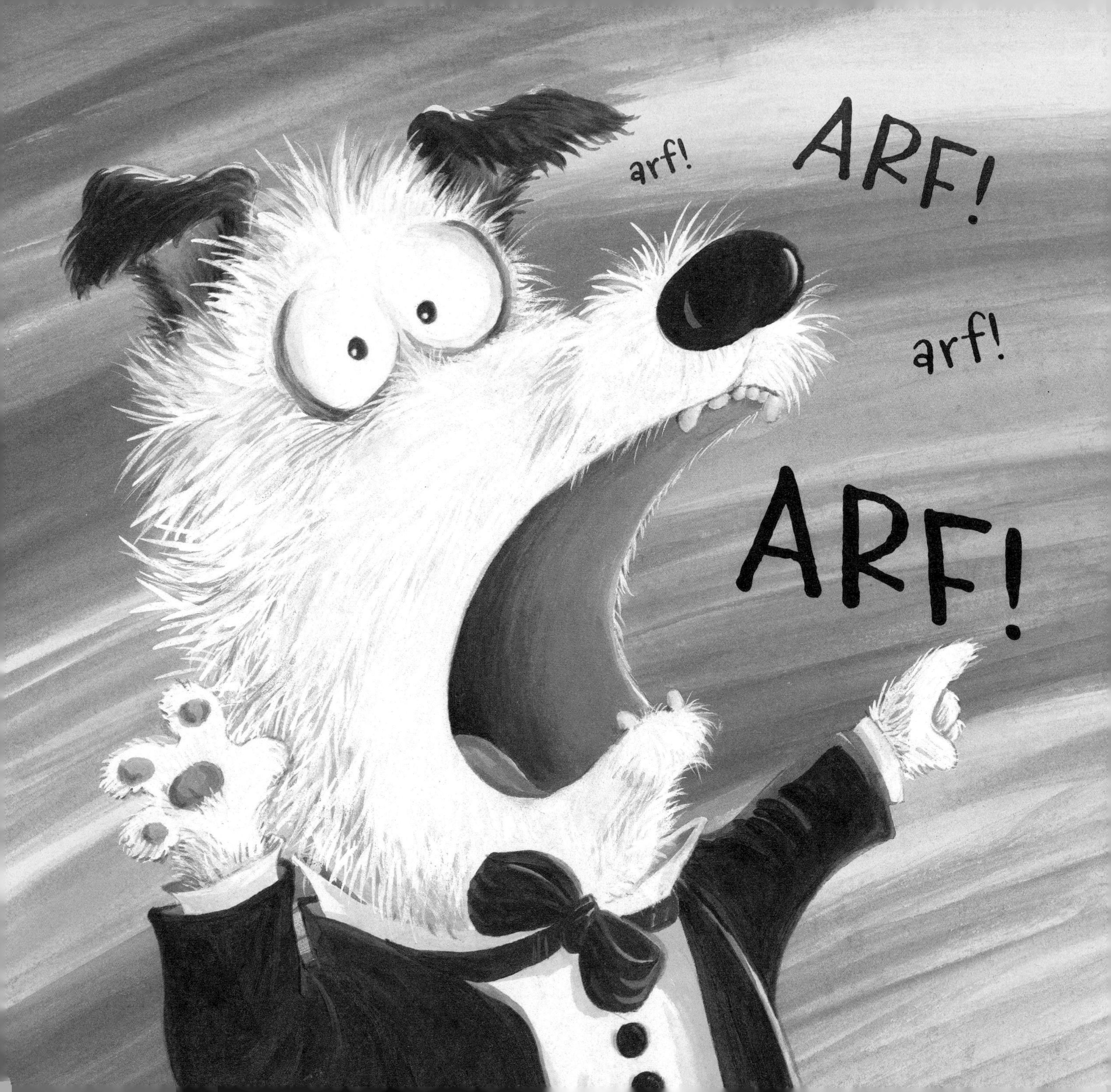
arf!
ARF!
arf!
ARF!

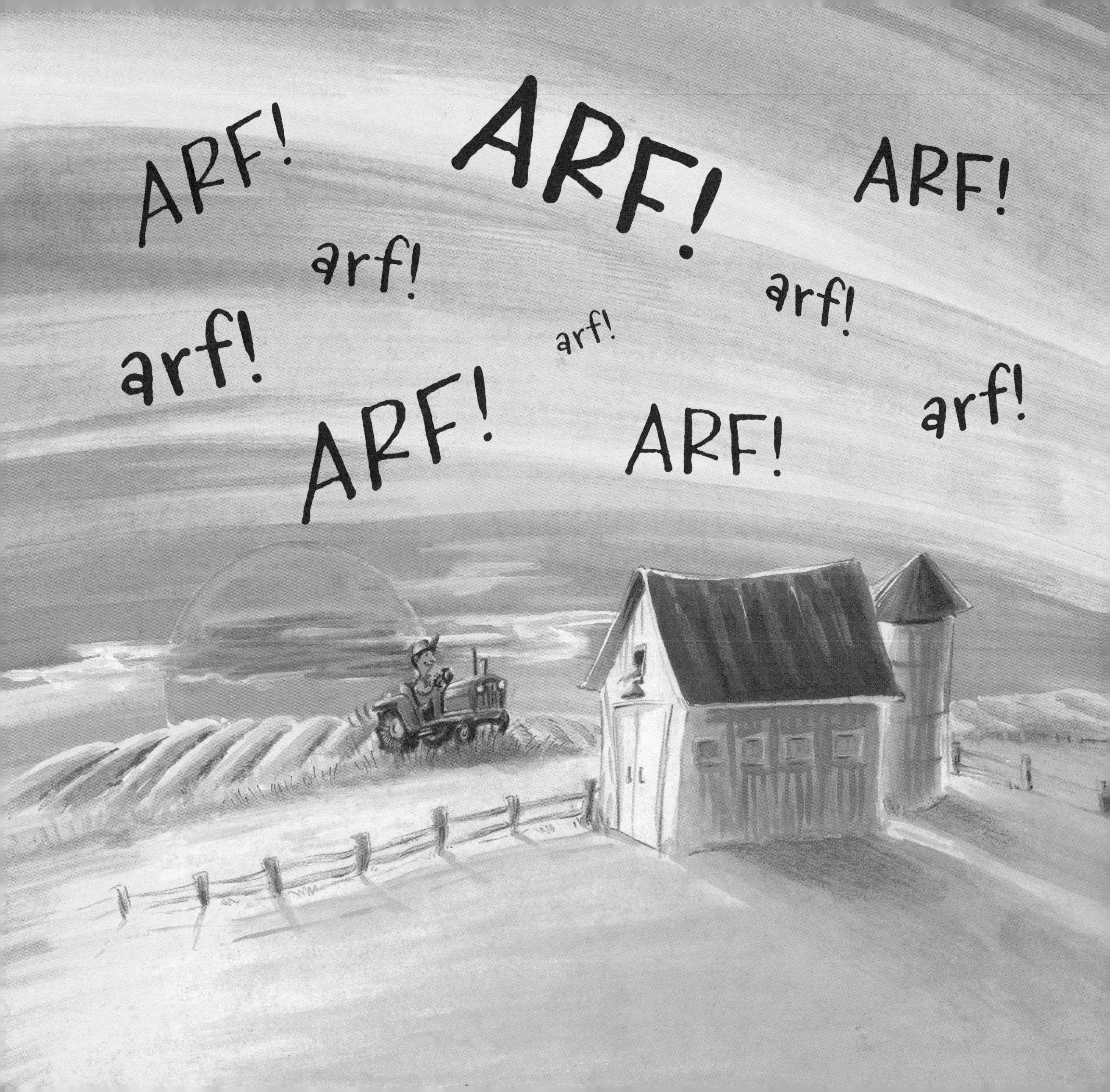
ARF!
ARF!
ARF!
arf!
arf!
arf!
arf!
arf!
ARF!
ARF!

shh shh shh shh
shh shh shhhhhhh

shh shh shh shh
shh shh shhhhhhh

eek!

arf

yap

neigh

baa

mew

quack

cluck

mama

moo

splish

splash

honk

tweet

cheep

bzz

sss

oink

ree

ribbet

eek

cock-a-doodle-doo